When I'm Gone

First passport photos

First lock of hair

One week old

Soon to be four!

Brighton

DEEP SEA CENTRE
SEASON TICKET

Fresh baby sister

Tenby at Easter

We LOVE sushi!

Happy Christmas!

Spring Barn Farm

1 x Child

Rufena, summer 2019

To my darling girls. All my love, Mama.
And to Dan. I love you.

And thank you to all the brilliant people at
Praxis für Hämatologie und Onkologie Berlin Mitte,
who have looked after me so well
M.M.

To my family, with love
H.W.

LADYBIRD BOOKS

UK | USA | Canada | Ireland | Australia
India | New Zealand | South Africa

Ladybird Books is part of the Penguin Random House group of companies
whose addresses can be found at global.penguinrandomhouse.com.

www.penguin.co.uk   www.puffin.co.uk   www.ladybird.co.uk

Penguin
Random House
UK

First published 2023
001

Printed in China
The authorized representative in the EEA is Penguin Random House Ireland,
Morrison Chambers, 32 Nassau Street, Dublin D02 YH68
A CIP catalogue record for this book is available from the British Library

ISBN: 978–0–241–52863–1

All correspondence to:
Ladybird Books Ltd
Penguin Random House Children's
One Embassy Gardens, 8 Viaduct Gardens
London SW11 7BW

When I'm Gone

Marguerite McLaren

Hayley Wells

Nobody lives forever.

Some people live a long, long life . . .

Like me.

When I am gone, remember me

and **all** the wonderful things

we did **together**

and the **happy** times we had.

When I am gone,
you will always
remember me.

And when I am gone,

I'll still love you
for ever and ever.

When I am gone,
please understand that
I didn't want to die.

I wish I could have
stayed with you
for longer.

To see you **grow** up.

To see you make
your way in life.

To hear about all your great adventures.

When I am gone,
you won't be alone.

You are so **loved**.

When I am gone,
you will have good days

and bad days.

It is OK to be sad

or angry

or confused.

When I am gone, it is also OK to be happy

and to have fun!

When I am gone,
your life goes on.

Live it!

Love it!

And even though I can't be
with you, my darlings,

I will **always** love you.
For ever and ever
and **ever**.

Don't Worry, Be Happy

Cousins!

SEPPI

Granny and Papa's garden

BRIGHTON to LONDON

RETURN TICKET

BERLIN

Happy 7ᵗʰ birthday!

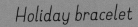

Holiday bracelet

SUNFLOWER

SEEDS

Supporting Bereaved Children

Children grieve just as much as adults, but they show it in different ways. They learn how to grieve by copying the responses of the adults around them and rely on adults to provide them with the support they need in their grief. Children have a limited ability to put feelings and thoughts into words and tend to show feelings with behaviours rather than words.

The following reactions are common:

- Picking up on tension and distress
- Appearing not to react
- Asking questions and exploring what death means
- Feeling anxious or insecure
- Feeling angry
- Looking after adults or feeling responsible
- Denying what has happened or taking risks

Every child is unique and will cope with the death of someone important in their own way. There is no magic formula but things that help include:

- Clear, honest and age-appropriate information
- Reassurance that they are not to blame and that different feelings are OK
- Normal routines and a clear demonstration that important adults are there for them
- Time to talk about what has happened, ask questions and build memories
- Being listened to and given time to grieve in their own way

You can find more support and guidance at **www.childbereavementuk.org**

Child Bereavement UK
REBUILDING LIVES TOGETHER